Behind the Scenes Christmas

Behind the Scenes
Christmas

Su Box

Illustrated by Jo Blake

Behind the Scenes Christmas

Abingdon Press

Published in the United States of America by Abingdon Press.
201 Eighth Avenue South, Nashville, Tennessee 37203

First edition 2006

First published by
ScriptureUnion, 207-209 Queensway, Bletchley, Milton Keynes, MK2 2EB, England.
www.scriptureunion.org.uk

Cover and internal design by Phil Grundy

ISBN 0-687-49121-5

06 07 08 09 10 11 12 13 14 15—10 9 8 7 6 5 4 3 2 1

Contents

Looking forward to Christmas

Are you looking forward to Christmas? Are you getting more excited as the big day draws near? Are you wondering if you'll receive the presents you've been hoping for?

Maybe it feels a long way off and you're getting impatient. It must have been like that for the Jewish people a little over two thousand years ago. They were waiting too – sometimes patiently, sometimes eagerly, and often wondering if anything was ever going to happen.

They weren't waiting for a special day but for a special person. They were looking forward to the arrival of the Messiah, God's promised king.

Many people were waiting, and some were listening faithfully to God. But only a few recognized the arrival of God's king – the best Christmas present ever.

You probably already know the name of this special king: Jesus. He's the reason we celebrate Christmas. You can find out why in this book, which takes a look "behind the scenes" at Christmas.

What does "Messiah" mean?

It is a Hebrew word meaning "the anointed one." (The Old Testament was written in Hebrew. In Old Testament times, Israelite kings had holy oil poured over the head. This was a sign that they had been set apart for the service of God. Anointing also showed that a person was being given the authority of God and the gift of his special power. In New Testament times, "Messiah" was translated as "Christ," which also means anointed.

Who were people expecting the Messiah to be?

At the time of Jesus, everyone had their own ideas about the Messiah. Many expected the Messiah to be a descendant of King David, the great king of Israel. One thousand years had passed since David became king.

Some people thought that the Messiah would be the perfect king, who would bring a time of peace and prosperity. Others thought he would overthrow the Romans who were occupying the land of Israel.

The Old Testament spoke of a leader who would come and rescue and save his people. When Jesus was born, many people thought it was time for these Old Testament prophecies to come true.

Who was Jesus?

When Jesus came, many people did realize that he was the Son of God and the Messiah they had been waiting for.

As they began to believe in and follow Jesus, they became known as Christians. Putting their trust in Jesus was a life-changing event for them. It's the same for people who come to know him as their friend and Savior today.

In the Old Testament, God used many different people to speak for God and their words were known as prophecies. People at the time of Jesus would have been familiar with those about the Messiah. Here are some of those prophecies about God's coming king: "You said, 'David, my servant, is my chosen one, and this is the agreement I made with him: David, one of your descendants will always be king.'" (Psalm 89:3–4)

"But the LORD will still give you proof.
A virgin is pregnant; she will have a son and will name him Immanuel." (In Hebrew this name means "God is with us". (Isaiah 7:14)
"A child has been born for us. We have been given a son who will be our ruler. His names will be Wonderful Advisor and Mighty God, Eternal Father and Prince of Peace. His power will never end; peace will last forever. He will rule David's kingdom and make it grow strong. He will always rule with honesty and justice. The LORD All-Powerful will make certain that all of this is done." (Isaiah 9:6–7)

Good News for Zechariah

Who are angels?

The Hebrew word for angel means "messenger" and this is the role of the angels in the Christmas story. It is said that when angels bring messages to people, God gives them a form similar to humans.

What did priests do?

Priests had many duties to perform with worshiping God and helping others to worship God too. These included teaching the Law (Torah), offering sacrifices to God and burning incense. They also did practical things such as looking after the collection of money in the temple.

Why was incense burned?

Burning incense – a mixture of ground spices – was a part of Jewish religious ritual. It symbolized offering prayer to God. Each morning and evening, and at special ceremonies, a priest would burn incense on a special altar beside the Holy Place (or Holy of Holies). Only priests were allowed into this part of the temple.

Luke 1:5-25, 57-80

Zechariah the priest was in the temple burning incense on the altar. All was quiet and still apart from the smoke rising and the muffled sound of people praying outside. Suddenly Zechariah realized that he was not alone.

Who had dared come into this holy place? Was it another priest? Zechariah was alarmed.

"Do not be afraid, Zechariah," said the stranger. "God has heard your prayer."

A message from God? Amazed, Zechariah realized that this was an angel.

"Your wife Elizabeth will give birth to a son. You are to name him John," the angel continued. "He will be filled with the Holy Spirit and he will prepare the people for the Lord's coming." Although Zechariah and Elizabeth were happy together, they had always longed for a child. Were their prayers about to be answered? Zechariah was doubtful.

"How can this be?" he asked. "I am old, and so is my wife Elizabeth."

"I am Gabriel. God sent me to give you good news," the angel said sternly. "But because you have not believed, you will not be able to speak until the child is born."

Everything happened just as the angel had said. Not only was Zechariah unable to speak, but before long his wife Elizabeth was pregnant.

Who was Gabriel?

The angel Gabriel is one of only two angels in the Bible who are named (the other is Michael). He is also mentioned in the Old Testament book of Daniel. The name Gabriel means "mighty man of God." Zechariah was struck dumb because he should have believed what Gabriel told him.

Why was childlessness a bad thing?

Sometimes life must have been difficult for Zechariah and Elizabeth because they had no children. In Zechariah's time children were seen as a blessing from God. People thought that God was punishing any married couple who didn't have a family.

Was Elizabeth unique?

In the Bible there are stories of other women who were childless for many years until God answered their prayers. The Old Testament tells of women who gave birth to sons with special roles, like Sarah, the mother of Isaac, and Hannah, the mother of Samuel.

Who was Zechariah's son?

Even before he was born, John's parents knew that he had something special to do for God. He was a prophet (someone who listens to God and tells other people what God has said). He was to help people to be ready to receive the Messiah. He became known as John the Baptist. This was because he baptized people in the River Jordan as a sign that they had changed their ways and were making a new start.

A Surprise for Mary

How old was Mary?

No one really knows, but she was probably in her early to mid teens. In New Testament times it was not unusual for a teenage girl to marry an older man. He would have had time to do well in his chosen trade or craft and would be able to provide a home for his new wife.

What did Mary do each day?

Girls were taught to be homemakers from childhood and Mary would have been busy with domestic tasks. It was hard work. Mary would have helped to grind grain into flour, cook food using a simple wood-burning oven, fetch water from the village well, wash clothes by hand, and sweep the hard-packed earth floor of the house.

Mary's song of praise

Later, Mary visited her cousin Elizabeth, the wife of Zechariah. The two women were full of wonder at the way God had blessed them. Mary trusted God. She was so happy, she sang a beautiful song which we often call "The Magnificat." You can read this in your Bible in Luke 1:46–55.

Luke 1:26-38

It was an ordinary day. Mary had been going about her everyday household tasks. She had been fetching water from the village well, sweeping the family's sleeping place, and helping her mother prepare food. Mary smiled to herself as she worked. She was thinking about Joseph, the man she was going to marry.

Mary was only a teenager but, as was the custom, she was already engaged to be married. Joseph the carpenter was a hard-working and caring man who could provide her with a good home.

Suddenly Mary sensed she was not alone. She looked up and gasped. There in front of her stood a stranger. He was tall, and quite unlike anyone she had seen before. Could this be an angel? Mary had heard about angels when the Scriptures were read at the synagogue.

"Don't be afraid, Mary," said the angel Gabriel. "God has chosen you to be the mother of a son. You will name him Jesus and he will be a great king."

"But how can this be?" asked Mary, confused. "I am not married."

"God will send God's Spirit upon you. Your child will be called the Son of God," Gabriel replied.

Mary was quiet for a moment – there were so many questions racing through her mind. Then she simply said, "I will do what God wants."

Was it an arranged marriage?

Parents usually chose the marriage partners for their sons and daughters. It was really important for a daughter to marry someone who could offer her security. It was the custom for the groom to give the bride's parents a payment or "bride price" for the daughter he had taken from them.

Why was Mary brave?

Mary could not be sure that Joseph would marry her when he heard her news. At this time it was shameful for an unmarried woman to have a child. Yet, although she was surprised, she hardly paused before humbly accepting God's plan.

What else do we know about Mary?

The Bible doesn't tell us much about her. But we know that she saw Jesus' first miracle, when he turned water into wine at a wedding. She knew his disciples. She was there when he died and, later met with Jesus' followers for worship and prayer.

Joseph's Strange Dream

Who was Joseph?

Joseph was a descendant of the great king of Israel, David. (You can read a list of his ancestors in Matthew 1:1–16.) By obeying the angel, Joseph made Mary's child his son, bringing Jesus into the family line of David. This fulfilled an Old Testament prophecy.

Could Joseph have divorced Mary?

Joseph and Mary were "bethrothed". This was rather like being engaged today but it was more serious. It could only be broken by an act of divorce. Joseph could have divorced Mary because she was pregnant and he was not the father of her baby.

Why use a dream?

In the Bible, if God had an important or urgent message to pass on, God sometimes used dreams or visions. And this happens several times in the Christmas story. Some other Bible characters whose lives were changed because of their dreams were Jacob, Joseph, Solomon, and Daniel.

Matthew 1:18-25

"An angel... chosen by God..." muttered Joseph as he tossed and turned.

It was hardly surprising that Joseph was sleeping badly. Mary, the young woman he was going to marry, had told him she was going to have a baby. Joseph knew he was not the child's father. She had told him a strange story about an angel telling her she was to be the mother of the Son of God. But how could Joseph believe that?

Angry and confused, Joseph had told Mary he needed time to think. That afternoon, he had hammered and sawed harder than usual.

By the time he had dozed off that night, Joseph had decided what to do. He could not marry Mary; why should he bring up a child who was not his own? No, he would quietly cancel their marriage plans. He was disappointed, but that was the way it would have to be.

"Joseph," a voice broke into his dreams. His dream was so real that it was as if a tall figure was standing in the room with him.

"Joseph, do not be afraid of taking Mary as your wife. What she told you is true..."

At last, Joseph slept peacefully.

Early the next day Joseph hurried to tell Mary the good news. Not only could their marriage take place, but he knew they would have God's blessing.

Why Jesus?

The angel told Joseph to call Mary's baby "Jesus," which means "God saves" because this would come true. Jesus would one day save the people of Israel, but not in the way they had expected. He died on the cross to save people from their wrongdoings.

What was Joseph's job?

Joseph was a carpenter in Nazareth. This was a skilled job. It would have involved a lot of building work, as well as tasks that could be carried out in the workshop attached to his home. Joseph would have made all sorts of items, from simple furniture to farming tools such as ploughs.

What else do we know about Joseph?

Unlike Mary, the Bible tells us nothing more about Joseph. He probably died before Jesus was grown up. But we do know that he taught his carpentry skills to Jesus, and that he and Mary went on to have several children.

The Journey to Bethlehem

What was the census?

The census which took Joseph and Mary to Bethlehem was planned by the Roman emperor Augustus. He wanted to make sure that everyone paid their taxes. So he said that everyone living in the Roman Empire must register – and be counted.

Why did Joseph and Mary go to Bethlehem?

People had to register in the town their family came from. Joseph's family was descended from King David, so he had to go to Bethlehem, where the king had been born. Mary went with him, as she was now part of his family.

Luke 2:1-5

"A census! Haven't the Romans caused us enough trouble already? We should be able to register at home in Nazareth," Joseph grumbled to Mary. She was riding on a donkey that he led carefully along the often bumpy road.

"Yes, it's a pity your family comes from Bethlehem and not from somewhere closer to Nazareth," agreed Mary. "But Emperor Augustus wants to be sure he doesn't miss out on any taxes."

"Taxes," said Joseph, "so they can build better roads, I hope!"

Mary and Joseph had been traveling for several days, sometimes alone and sometimes in the company of other travelers, for safety. At night they had slept as best they could by the roadside. During the day they stopped frequently for Mary to rest.

Joseph could see that Mary was very tired. It was hardly surprising, for her baby was expected soon. The afternoon sun was low in the sky when Joseph spotted the little hilltop town of Bethlehem.

"Look! The city of David," Joseph said, reassuringly. "We'll soon be there."

Mary smiled. She was relieved that their journey would soon be at an end. She was glad that they would have somewhere comfortable to stay that night. She had a feeling it wouldn't be long before her baby was born.

How long was their journey?

The distance between Nazareth and Bethlehem is about sixty-eight miles. Nazareth was high on a hill. Mary and Joseph probably journeyed down into and along the valley of the River Jordan to Jerusalem, and then south to the town of Bethlehem.

Was there a donkey?

The Bible doesn't say how Mary and Joseph traveled. However, people would often cover such a distance on foot. As Mary was pregnant, it is highly likely that she would have ridden on a donkey. Joseph would have walked alongside.

Would they have traveled alone?

At the time of Jesus traveling could be dangerous. Thieves and robbers often lay in wait in lonely places. There might be fierce wild animals too. Joseph and Mary might have joined another group of travelers or, at least, kept them in sight for safety.

What were the taxes used for?

The Roman emperor's government kept law and order throughout the Roman Empire. It also made some of the best roads ever built, and provided many fine public buildings. These were paid for with money raised from taxes paid by local people.

No Room at the Inn

What was the inn like?

A Middle-Eastern inn wasn't like a modern hotel. It might have had a central courtyard for the animals with stalls on all sides where travelers could rest. The innkeeper would provide a fire for everyone to use for cooking.

Was it a stable?

Christmas cards often show a wooden stable. But according to tradition this might have been a cave used for housing animals. Jesus was laid in a manger, a trough usually used for the animals' food. So animals might have been there. The manger might even have been carved into the wall of the cave.

Or a house?

It is also possible that Mary and Joseph were offered shelter in a family home. Sometimes, especially in the homes of poor families, animals and people had to live under the same roof. There were no separate rooms, but the family slept on a raised platform apart from the animals.

Luke 2:5-7

"You're too late."

"We've no room."

It was the same everywhere. Joseph hadn't expected so many strangers to be in Bethlehem for the census.

He was getting worried. It was nearly dusk and Mary needed to rest after their long journey.

At last one man noticed the tired young woman who was very pregnant. His answer was: "We've no room.

But wait... You'd have to share with the animals."

Joseph glanced toward Mary.

"All we need is somewhere dry to shelter us from the night air," he said with a smile. "That's very kind. Thank you."

Later that night, in the animals' shelter, Mary gave birth to their son. She was far away from everything she had prepared at home... and far from the crib that Joseph had made so lovingly. Instead he had hastily cleaned out a manger, an animals' feeding trough, and filled it with clean soft straw – a makeshift bed for a new king.

At last Mary and Joseph rested. They were thankful for their strange shelter and full of all the love and wonder of new parents. To them baby Jesus couldn't be any more special.

What animals were there?

The Bible doesn't mention any animals in the Nativity story but it's possible that some were present. People of that time might have kept a cow or ox (used for pulling a plough) and a donkey. There might also be sheep or goats, often left grazing outside. There wouldn't have been any pigs as these are unclean animals to followers of the Jewish faith.

What did baby Jesus wear?

Mary would have wrapped Jesus in swaddling clothes. These were nothing like the modern baby clothes used today. The custom was to wrap a newborn baby snug in a soft blanket. Then they would use long strips of cloth – swaddling bands – to hold the baby safe and secure.

Who would have helped Mary give birth?

It was usual for the mother to arrange with an older woman to act as "midwife." The father would not be at the birth. However, as newly-arrived strangers, Mary and Joseph might not have been able to follow tradition. Perhaps a woman where they were staying helped out.

In what year was Jesus born?

We sometimes add BC or AD to dates so that we know if something happened "Before Christ" or "After Christ" (Anno Domini or "in the year of our Lord" in Latin). In fact, Jesus wasn't born exactly between 1 BC and AD 1 but probably a few years earlier. (The date was calculated wrongly in the Middle Ages.)

Why did the angels visit shepherds?

It is interesting that God chose ordinary people to be the first to hear the good news about the birth of Jesus. When Jesus grew up, he showed that he had come to serve everyone. No one was too humble for Jesus to love, and everyone was invited to take a place in his kingdom.

Why were the shepherds out at night?

Sheep were allowed to graze freely during the day. At night they may have been gathered into a sheepfold (an enclosure) for safety. The shepherds would sleep across the entrance to the fold so that they were able to protect the sheep from wild animals.

What did the shepherds do?

Without knowing it, the shepherds were the first witnesses to Jesus. Having heard that their Savior had been born, they hurried to see this new baby. Anyone they met on the way to or from Bethlehem must have been amazed at their story.

Jesus, shepherds, and sheep

Sheep play an important part in Jesus' life. They remind us that he is descended from King David, who had been a shepherd in Bethlehem. They also remind us that Jesus asks Christians to follow him, just as sheep follow their shepherd even today (John 10:4).

An Exciting Night

Luke 2:8-20

Out in the chill night air on hills not far from Bethlehem, some shepherds were taking care of their sheep. The shepherds dozed, chatted softly, and occasionally threw some wood onto their fire. The night was clear and still. Suddenly the dark night sky shone with a bright light, brighter than the most brilliant star.

"What is it?" cried one shepherd in alarm. Terrified, they shielded their eyes against the light.

"Do not be afraid," said a voice. "I have brought good news for you and for all people."

Good news? The shepherds looked up, now curious and a little less fearful. And there before them, bathed in a shining light, was an angel!

"Your Savior has been born in David's town. You will find him lying in a manger."

Suddenly the sky was filled with a great choir of angels singing praises to God.

When the angels had gone, the shepherds left their flock and hurried off to Bethlehem. They were leaping and shouting with excitement!

The shepherds had quieted down by the time they reached the stable. Peeping inside they saw a sleepy father and mother tending a newborn child. It was just as the angel had told them. Quietly, shyly, they went inside. Full of wonder, they knelt down and worshiped the newborn king of the world.

Jesus as a good shepherd

At the time of Jesus, shepherds had to take great care of their sheep. Jesus later described himself as the good shepherd. His hearers would have understood that he was going to love and care for his "sheep" (or followers) (John 10:11).

Jesus as a lamb

Part of Jewish religious practice at this time was to bring a perfect lamb to sacrifice at the temple. This was a way for someone to say they were sorry and to pay for their wrongdoings. Jesus was later called the "Lamb of God" because he died to take away our sins (things that we have said or done that have hurt God and others).

Was Jesus born in wintertime?

The shepherds and their sheep were out on the hillside. So Jesus could not have been born in December – mid-winter in the northern hemisphere. In fact, we do not know the date of Jesus' birth. Christians began celebrating his birthday on December 25 in the fourth century, to replace a Roman pagan festival.

Simeon's Wonderful Day

Why did Mary and Joseph visit the Temple?

Joseph and Mary took baby Jesus to the Temple in Jerusalem for an important religious reason. They would have offered a sacrifice – probably two doves or pigeons – so that Mary could be declared "clean" after giving birth.

What else did they have to do?

As the firstborn son, Jesus was believed to belong to God in a special way. He had to be "redeemed" (bought back) from God by the payment of five pieces of silver. This was done in memory of God sparing the oldest sons of the Israelites at the time of the Exodus (when the Israelites left Egypt, where they had been slaves. You can read all about the Exodus in the Old Testament book of that name).

Who was Simeon?

Simeon was one of the few Jews who had a true understanding of the sort of Savior (or rescuer) the coming Messiah would be. As a reward for his faith, God had promised Simeon that he would not die before seeing the Messiah.

Luke 2:22-35

Simeon had been a friend of God for long enough to recognize the voice of God's Spirit. Long ago, God had told Simeon he would not die before he had seen the Messiah. Today that same voice had told him to go to the Temple.

Arriving at the Temple, Simeon noticed a couple with a young baby entering the courtyard. They must have come to make a thanksgiving sacrifice and to offer the child back to God as the Jewish law required.

Something made Simeon go up to them. And then he knew – this was no ordinary baby, this was the long-awaited Messiah!

"May I hold him?" asked Simeon, eagerly.

Mary smiled and handed her precious baby to the old man.

"Lord, now let your servant die in peace, for I have seen your salvation," said Simeon. He was full of joy and wonder as he gave thanks to God for keeping God's promise. Simeon blessed Mary and Joseph and handed Jesus back to them. Then, he looked serious. He told Mary that she would know sadness when Jesus did what God had planned for him.

Mary and Joseph were amazed. It seemed that this old man knew more about their son than they did! But right now they were too happy to worry about the future.

What did Simeon say?

Simeon was given the gift of prophecy when he spoke to Mary. He listened to what God had to say about Jesus, and told Mary what he heard. He talked about what Jesus had come to do for Israel. But he also warned Mary that sorrow lay ahead of her because of what people would do to her son.

What was the significance of the Temple?

The site of the Jerusalem Temple was a piece of land that King David had bought from a farmer on the hill of Zion. For the people of Israel the temple was a symbol of God's presence among them. It was the center of religious life for the Jews.

Who built the Temple?

King Solomon built the first Temple but this was destroyed over five hundred years earlier. Now King Herod had overseen the building of a new Temple (the third on the same site). It took about ten years to build. It was a huge limestone building with marble pillars, golden gates and colorful wall hangings.

Why did people make sacrifices?

At the time of Jesus' birth, people made offerings or sacrifices of different sorts – grain, part or all of an animal, or money. These might be, for example, to give thanks to God, to seek peace or to ask for forgiveness. However, they had no lasting value, unlike the sacrifice Jesus later made on the cross. All the things we've done wrong hurt God and break our relationship with God. By dying for us, Jesus took the wrong things away and made us right with God forever.

Following a Star

What was the star?

No one knows for sure. Some people believe that the wise men's "star" might have been an exploding star, or supernova. This would have been very bright. Others say that it might have been a comet. But it behaved very strangely for any kind of "ordinary" star. So it could have been a unique and special sign from God.

Were the wise men kings?

The men must have been important because mighty King Herod was willing to meet them. But the Bible does not tell us that they were kings themselves, only that they were searching for the King of kings.

Why are they called "wise" men?

They were probably given the name "wise men" (or "Magi") because they made a special study of the planets. This was a skilled job. They would have learned all about the position of different constellations of stars throughout the year.

"A new star! It's the sign we've been waiting for!" the man had called out excitedly. "Surely this will lead us to the King of kings!"

The wise men had been watching the skies for this special sign for many years. Now their patience had been rewarded. Soon they were on their way, their camels laden with all that they might need for a long journey. And, carefully hidden in their packs, there were some very precious gifts.

After many weeks following the star, they began to wonder… "Will we ever find the king? Perhaps we should visit the next palace?" And so they did. It was the palace of a king called Herod.

At first King Herod seemed surprised when they asked about the new king. But then he told them of ancient prophecies about a king being born in Bethlehem.

So the men set off once more.

At long last the star stopped its journey – and so did the wise men. They dismounted, tied up their camels, and rummaged in their packs.

There was no palace, just some ordinary houses. But through an open doorway, they could see a mother with a toddler on her lap. This child must be the new king. They had found him at last!

Eagerly, the men went into the house and knelt before the mother and child. And then they brought out the gifts they had carried with them. Precious gifts of gold, frankincense, and myrrh – gifts fit for a king.

Were there three?

No one knows for sure. Tradition says that there were three wise men. This is because they brought three gifts – gold, frankincense, and myrrh. But there could have been more. As they were clearly well off, they might have taken some servants with them.

Did their gifts have any meaning?

Since early church times, people have thought that the wise men's gifts were symbols of Jesus and what he had come to do. Gold honored him as king. Frankincense (used in worship) recognized he was God. And myrrh (used during burial) pointed to his death. It seems that the wise men knew more than they actually said.

Was their visit significant?

The shepherds remind us that Jesus came for all people, both rich and poor. In the same way, the wise men's visit had other meanings too. They bowed before Jesus, offering him honor and worship.

They recognized that he had come to humanity as a king. They also showed that Jesus was important for Gentiles (non-Jewish people), because the wise men were not Jews.

Where did they come from?

The Bible tells us only that the wise men came from the East. At that time traders traveled from places then called Persia, Babylon and Arabia. They would often bring with them spices and fine fabrics.

An Escape by Night

Which Herod?

The Bible mentions several rulers from the Herod family. They all seem to have been unpleasant characters. When Jesus was born, Herod the Great was king. It was his son, Herod Antipas, who agreed to the killing of Jesus about thirty-three years later.

Who was Herod?

The Romans appointed Herod the Great king of the Jews, although he was only partly Jewish. He was an unpopular leader, and he lived in continual fear of a rebellion. He was always quick to destroy anyone who might be a rival.

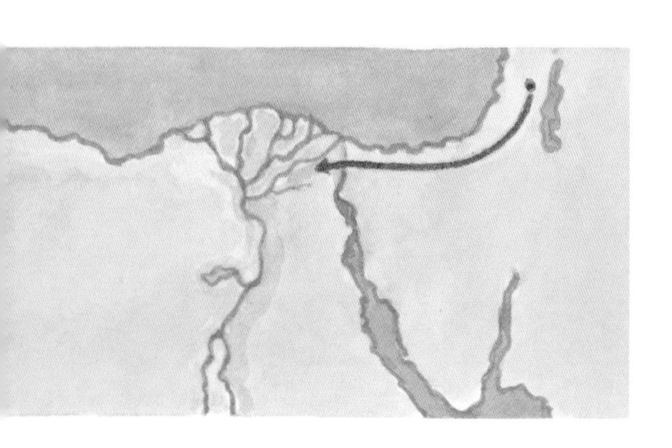

What route did they take?

Joseph and Mary's long journey to Egypt would have first taken them south. Then it would have taken them west, somewhere across the Negev Desert and Sinai Peninsula. On their journey they might have gone along some of the route taken by Moses (Israel's great leader in the Old Testament) as he traveled toward the Promised Land about fifteen hundred years earlier.

Matthew 2:12-16

"A new king!" muttered Herod, angrily. "I am the king. No one is going to take my place."

The visit of the wise men had worried Herod. Was this part of another plot to overthrow him? Just in case, he had told the visitors from the east that he too would like to worship the child. They would tell him where the child was to be found and then Herod could get rid of him.

Days passed and the men did not return. Herod brooded and planned. He did not know that God had warned the wise men not to return to the palace.

When Herod found out that the wise men were not coming back, he was very angry. At last he decided what

to do. He would order his soldiers to kill any baby boys in Bethlehem who were younger than 2 years old. Then he would be sure that this new king would never come to power. Herod laughed. It was simple!

But that same night an angel spoke to Joseph in a dream. "Herod wants to kill Jesus. You must escape to Egypt and stay there until it is safe."

"Quickly, we must leave," Joseph said, shaking Mary awake and telling her the terrible news.

He loaded some important clothes and possessions onto their donkey. Then, while the moon was still high in the sky, they set off on their long journey to safety.

How long did they stay away?

Mary and Joseph must have spent two or three years in Egypt. Then Joseph was given another angelic message in a dream. This time it was good news. He was told that Herod was dead and that it was safe to return to Nazareth.

What happened next?

As a carpenter, Joseph could have found work in Egypt. The family returned to their home in southern Galilee when Herod died and it was safe. This time, they took care to avoid Bethlehem on their long journey. Little is known about Jesus' childhood but he was probably brought up as an ordinary village boy. He would have learned his father's trade and attended the synagogue (the place where Jews worship). The Bible next mentions Jesus when he was 12 years old.

Why did people travel to Egypt?

From earliest times people had traveled between the two countries. With no sea between them it was an easy, if long, journey. The most common reason was for trade. But at times of famine the people of Israel might go to the more fertile land around the River Nile.

Good News!

At the heart of our Christmas celebrations is the amazing fact that God became a child. God was born into our world as the baby Jesus. The angels announced this as good news of great joy for all people. And that good news wasn't just for people living at the time of Jesus, but for all time – and that includes you, today!

Why celebrate?

Christians celebrate Christmas not only because of Jesus' birth – that's only part of the story. It's also because of who he was. Jesus came to show people how to live as God wanted. He also came as our Savior, so that all the wrong things we do can be forgiven. When he died, he made us right with God. If we love and trust Jesus, nothing will come between us and God.

Where does the word "Christmas" come from?

In New Testament times the Hebrew word for "anointed" (remember, this is what "Messiah" means) began to be translated into the Greek language as "Christ." "Christmas" comes from the Old English "Christes maesse" which means the Mass of Christ – "mass" meaning a time of celebration.

The End of the Story?

Mary and Joseph's escape to Egypt marks the end of the stories we think about at Christmas time. The Christmas story is wonderful – miraculous and exciting.

But the events of the first couple of years of Jesus' life weren't the end. Do you remember, the Jews were looking forward to the coming of a Messiah?

The shepherds, the wise men, and Simeon were some of a small group of people who knew that little baby Jesus was someone really special – God's promised King.

Over the years, Mary must have thought about the events of that first Christmas: the angels, the unexpected visitors, and what Simeon had said to her. She knew that Jesus was the Son of God and the long-awaited Messiah who had come to save his people. But what did that mean?

Did she guess what was in store for her much-loved son? But that's another chapter of the unforgettable story that begins at Christmas...

Why do we give Christmas presents?

Wherever you live, there are different traditions about giving gifts at Christmas. Many people say it's a tradition based on the wise men bringing gifts. Whatever the reason, it's good to remember that Christmas isn't all about what you get. It's a time when we celebrate God's gift of love to us – Jesus. And, by giving gifts to others, we share our love with them.

What is Epiphany?

You may see this word in diaries or calendars on January 6. This Greek word means "to show" or "make known." It is linked with Jesus being shown to the wise men. In Spain, this is known as "Three Kings Day." It's an alternative time for gift giving.

What other names are given to Jesus?

In the Bible many different names are given to Jesus. Some are found in Old Testament prophecies. Some were said by Jesus himself. Some were spoken by people who recognized who he was. How many of them do you know already? Isaiah 9:6–7 is a good place to start! (See page 9.)